Based on the TV series *Rugrats®* created by Arlene Klasky, Gabor Csupo, and
Paul Germain as seen on Nickelodeon®

No part of this publication may be reproduced in whole or in part, or stored in a
retrieval system, or transmitted in any form or by any means, electronic,
mechanical, photocopying, recording, or otherwise, without written permission of the
publisher. For information regarding permission, write to Simon Spotlight,
an imprint of Simon & Schuster Children's Publishing Division,
1230 Avenue of the Americas, New York, NY 10020.

ISBN 0-439-11535-3

12 11 10 9 8 7 6 5 4 3 2 1   9/9 0 1 2 3 4/0

Printed in the U.S.A.   23

First Scholastic printing, September 1999

UP AND AWAY, REPTAR!

By Sarah Willson
Illustrated by Cary Rillo

SCHOLASTIC INC.
New York   Toronto   London   Auckland   Sydney
Mexico City   New Delhi   Hong Kong

It was the day of the big Reptar fair and parade.
Everyone was there!

"We're gonna carry the Reptar balloon, Chuckie," said Tommy.
"Are you excited?"

"Not really," said Chuckie.

"I invented this baby float,"
Stu proudly told Chas.
"See? It has a little motor. The kids sit
here—there's even a place for Dil.
Then they all can hold the balloon strings."

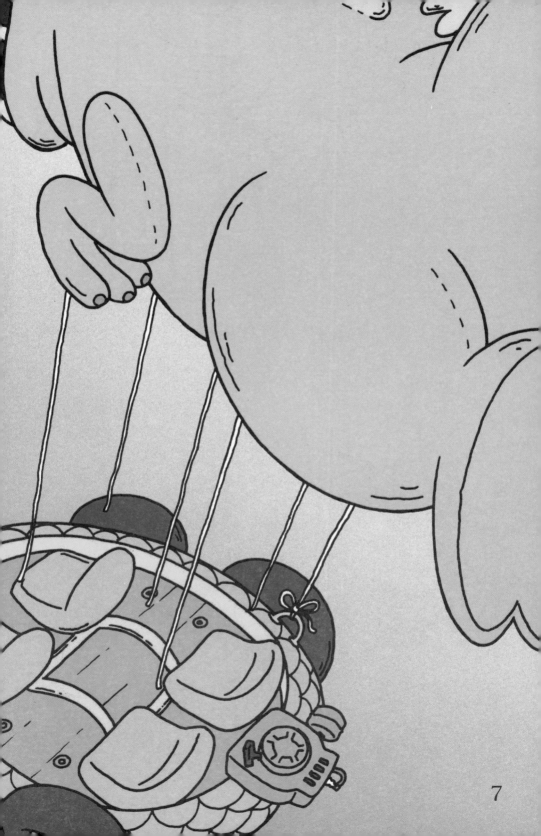

Stu and Chas put the babies onto the float.

"Uh, shouldn't that valve be closed?" asked Chas.

But Stu didn't hear him.

"Didi will be marching with the kids,"Stu said.

"Let's go to the finish line so we can take a picture of them!"

"Stu will be marching with the kids,"
Didi told Betty.

"Let's go to the finish line so we can
be there to cheer for them!"

The parade was about to begin.
"This is great!" yelled Tommy.
Chuckie wasn't so sure.
"Isn't there supposed to be a
growed-up marching with us?"
he asked.

Slowly the babies began to float
into the air.

"Hey!" said Phil.
"My feet aren't touching anything!"

"Don't worry," said Tommy.
"Reptar knows where we're going.
Maybe he wants to surprise us."

No one noticed the babies floating away.

"I hear a whooshing sound!" said Phil.

"It feels like we're going down," said Lil.

"I don't know about this, Tommy," Chuckie said.

"Reptar knows the way," said Tommy.

The balloon came down.
It landed on top of a big truck.
"See?" said Tommy.
"Reptar put us on this truck
to take us to the surprise."

The babies let go of
the balloon strings.
But Dil did not.

They watched Reptar carry Dil away.
"Where's Dil going?" asked Lil.
"It's Dil's naptime," said Tommy.
"Reptar knows you gotta keep moving
so Dil will fall asleep."

The truck drove to the fair.
The babies climbed down from the truck.
"I told you Reptar had a surprise for us!" cried Tommy.

"Reptar bars!" yelled the babies.
Sure enough, Reptar was giving out
candy bars.

The babies ate a lot.
Then they heard a shout.

"There they are!"
It was Stu, Didi, Betty, and Chas.
They rushed over to pick up the babies.
"But . . . WHERE IS DIL?" wailed Didi.

Meanwhile, Dil and the Reptar balloon floated gently.

Zzzzzz went the sleeping baby.

Whoosh went the leaky air valve.

The balloon landed on a train.

Kiddie Line

"THERE HE IS!" boomed Betty.
She pointed to the train ride.
The grown-ups rushed over.

"See?" said Tommy.
"Reptar just put Dil down
for his nap. He knows Dil is too little
to eat Reptar bars."

The babies stuffed their diapers
with Reptar bars.
Then they joined Dil on the train.
"We forgot to thank Reptar," said Chuckie.
"Don't worry, Chuckie," said Tommy.
"Reptar knows."